THE YUMS

Broccoli was having
a really bad day

The soles of his feet
were turning quite grey

That can happen
to Broccoli over time

He can lose his freshness
and his toes turn to slime

Broccoli needed a plan
to maintain his crunch

so people would want
to eat him for lunch

He thought he would
try jogging

Staying fit was his dream

But his purple shorts
made Strawberry scream!

'I'll stay cool in the fridge'
He said to himself

and he wore his sunglasses
on the top shelf

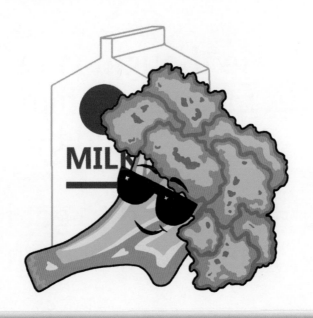

He thought yoga
might keep him
in peek condition

but struggled to get into
the lotus position

To stay moisturised
Broccoli oiled his hair

He was drippy and
slippy

but he didn't care

Hooray for Broccoli!

At the end of the day

he showed no sign of
drooping, slime or decay

Created by Mary Ingram.

Read about Broccoli's friends ...

strawberry

www.theyums.co.uk

Potato

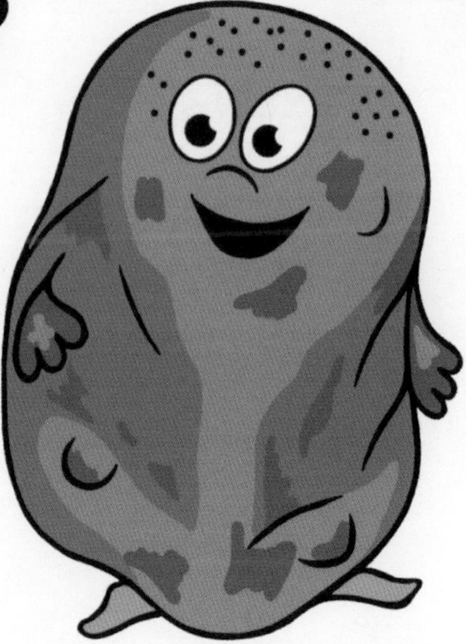

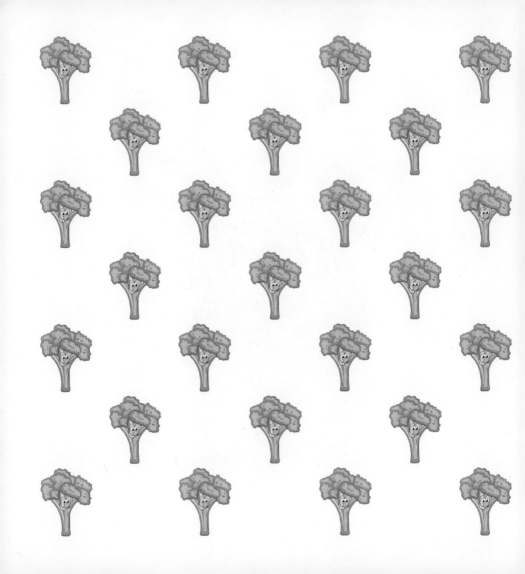

Printed in Great Britain
by Amazon